THANK YOU,
MY DEAR READER
FOR CHOOSING THIS

Illustrator: Alyona Rychagova
Author: Alex Fabller

MORE BOOKS AT

scan me

ALEXFABLER.COM

When the sun fell asleep with a smile on its face
and allowed the Moon to take its place,
all the sleepyheads were getting ready for bed
except for little Lisa in pajamas painted red.

Lying in bed, she watched the starry sky.
"I wish I were an astronaut," she said with a sigh.
So she stared at the Moon, bright in grace,
hoping that one day she would visit space.

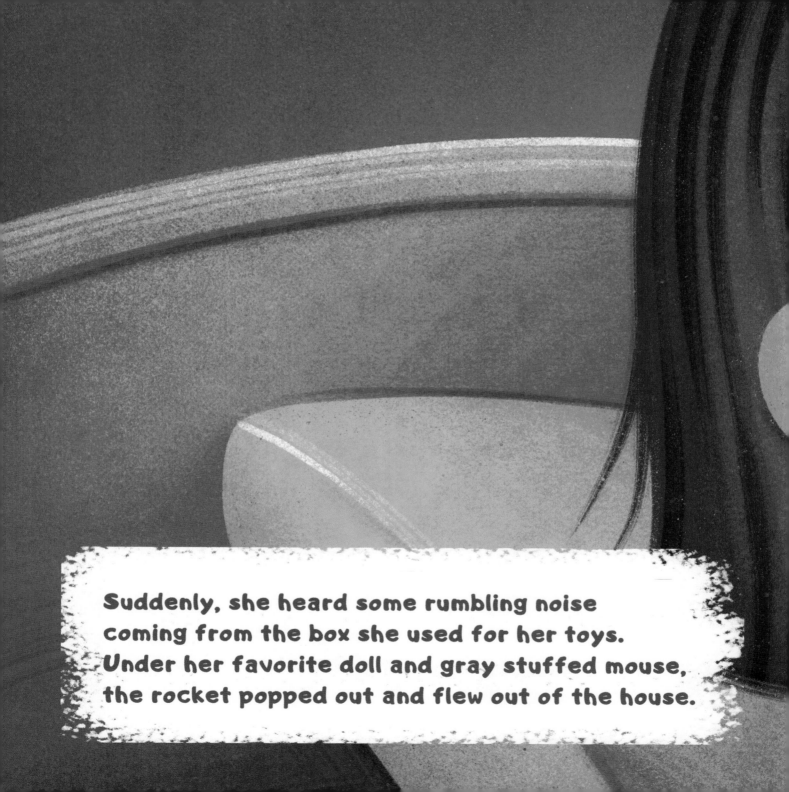

Suddenly, she heard some rumbling noise
coming from the box she used for her toys.
Under her favorite doll and gray stuffed mouse,
the rocket popped out and flew out of the house.

Looking out the window, Lisa rubbed her eyes.
The rocket was in her yard. What a surprise!
She hurried downstairs, toward the door
as the giant-sized rocket made a loud roar.

She fastened her seat belt as she stepped inside,
knowing it would be a long and bumpy ride.
She pressed the button, ready to fly so high.
The rocket took off towards the starry sky.

She was among space objects of every kind.
So fast and noisy, Lisa left the Earth behind.
And just like that, after all that rush,
her flight became calm, soothing, and hush.

Lisa heard the swoosh of the lost meteorite,
passing by her drowsy eyes at the speed of light.
The rocket was rocking like a light sweep.
Even the planets were getting ready to sleep.

Lisa saw Mercury, the closest to the sun,
so rocky and gray and the smallest one.
It glanced at Lisa so tiny as a midge
and lulled its surface as cold as a fridge.

Venus was spinning opposite the Earth,
preparing its cozy sleeping place with mirth.
With clouds as soft as a comfy pillow,
its magical dreams are about to billow.

The planet Earth appeared in her line of sight.
Blue as a marble with swirls painted white.
Sleepy and tired, making a small peep,
until Lisa returns, Earth won't fall asleep.

And just around the corner, shining so bright,
Lisa spotted Earth's natural satellite.
The moon followed the Earth all around
so we could see it at night from the ground.

Flying next to the shining and twinkling stars,
Lisa saw the Red Planet known as Mars.
Red rocks and dust were sleeping soundly.
Even the spacecraft was snoring loudly.

The Mighty Jupiter, decorated with stripes,
covered with clouds and storms of all types,
rubbed its eyes and turned off the light,
wishing little Lisa a peaceful good night.

Unique and made mostly of gas,
Saturn stood there in all its mass.
With beautiful rings shining in the night,
Saturn whispered softly, "Sleep tight."

Lisa continued her journey full of fun
and saw the seventh planet from the sun.
Rotating so slowly, a giant in size,
Uranus closed his sleepy blue eyes.

And there in the distance, like colorful balloons,
Neptune was sleeping with his 14 Moons.
Nothing could wake this beautiful blue gin,
snoring with the winds that blow and spin.

Lisa was as sleepy as she had ever been
but happy for beauties she had never seen.
And just when she turned the rocket back,
she saw something shy on the star track.

It was Pluto, cold and filled with ice,
yawning and rubbing its reddish eyes.
This dwarf planet looked at Lisa and said,
"It's time to go to bed, you sleepy head."

Indeed, Lisa has turned her spaceship,
ready to end this magical trip.
Flying among the stardust and the space dome,
she could hardly wait to return to her home.

Without stopping, she was hurrying ahead;
and landed from the rocket right into her bed.
She closed her eyes as bright as two beams
because anything is possible in Lisa's dreams.

Thank you, my dear readers, for choosing this book!

If you have an opinion about this book, don't keep it inside. Share it with the world around you. Maybe after that the world will be a little happier!

amazon.co.uk

amazon.com

amazon.ca

Printed in Great Britain
by Amazon

18583834R00025